This book belongs to

_____

Disney's
Beauty and the Beast

A Read-Aloud Storybook

Adapted by Ellen Titlebaum

MOUSE WORKS

Find us at www.disneybooks.com for more Mouse Works fun!

Printed in the United States.

ISBN: 0-7364-0125-3

THE SPELL IS CAST

One winter's eve, a beggar offered the Prince a red rose in return for shelter. He sneered at her gift, and turned her away.

"Do not be deceived by appearances," the beggar warned, revealing that she was an enchantress!

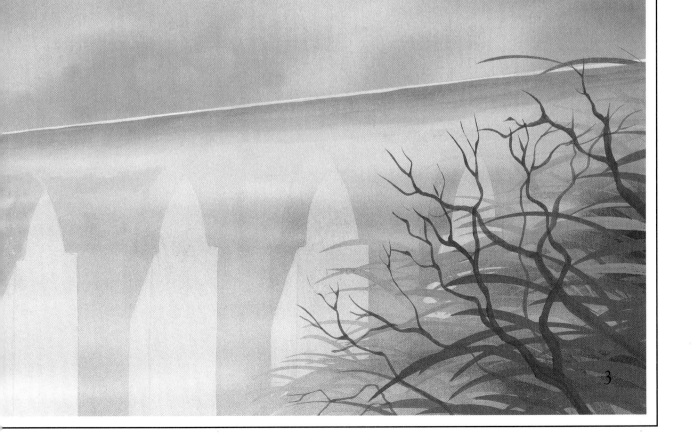

The Enchantress turned the Prince into a hideous beast, and placed a spell on everyone in the castle. She left behind only the rose she had offered him.

For the spell to be broken, the Prince would have
to love another and earn that person's love in return
before the rose's last petal fell.

Belle lived in a village near the castle. She loved to read books about adventure and romance.

One morning, Gaston the hunter saw Belle and boasted, "That's the girl I'm going to marry."

At Belle's house, her father, Maurice, was working on a new invention.

"You'll win first prize at the fair tomorrow," predicted Belle.

But Maurice and his horse Philippe never made it to the fair. They became lost in the dark forest.

Black bats flew out of the shadows, followed by growling wolves. The terrified horse threw his rider off and charged into the woods.

Maurice ran down a hillside, crashing into branches and toppling over gigantic roots until he saw an old gate in front of a castle.

He forced the gate open and escaped just before the wolves reached him!

Maurice approached the castle, and stepped inside. "Not a word," whispered Cogsworth, the clock, to Lumiere, the candelabrum. The people in the castle had been changed into enchanted objects!

Friendly Lumiere announced, "Welcome, Monsieur!"

Suddenly, a huge beast stormed into the room.
"A stranger!" the Beast growled.

Huge, clawed hands grabbed Maurice and took him to the dungeon!

At that very moment, Gaston had arrived at Belle's house to propose marriage. A crowd waited outside to celebrate.

"Say you'll marry me," he ordered. Belle refused. She did not like the conceited bully!

When the crowd had left, Philippe arrived, with no rider.

"Philippe! Where's Papa? You must take me to him!" cried Belle.

BELLE'S PROMISE

Belle rode through the forest, braving the thick fog and frightening sounds. Soon she saw the huge turrets and gates of the castle rising out of the mist.

When Belle entered the castle, she found her father locked in the dungeon. As they embraced, a voice boomed from the shadows.

"I am the master of this castle!" roared the Beast.

"Take me instead," Belle cried.

When Belle promised to stay with the Beast forever, he released Maurice.

The Beast showed Belle to her room. "You can go anywhere you like . . . except the west wing. You'll join me for dinner," said the Beast and then he was gone.

Belle was angry at the Beast's unkind treatment. Not even Mrs. Potts, the friendly teapot, could cheer her up.

In the dining room, the Beast waited for Belle to join him for dinner.

"Master," said Lumiere, "this girl could be the one to break the spell! You fall in love and . . ."

"She'll always see me as a monster," grumbled the Beast.

Back in the village, Maurice begged for help to rescue Belle from a horrible beast. The crowd laughed, convinced that he was crazy.

But Gaston was thinking up a terrible plan.

At the castle, Belle had skipped dinner and was now hungry.

"Be our guest," said Lumiere, leading Belle to the dining room. Bottles popped their corks, dishes danced, and serving pieces carried in tasty food!

After dinner, Belle wandered into the forbidden west wing and found the enchanted rose.

She was about to touch it when the Beast shouted, "Get out!"

Terrified, Belle fled the castle and rode Philippe into the night.

Spooky yellow eyes glowed in the dark forest.
The wolves were right behind them, lunging at
Philippe's hooves. Belle was thrown off and tumbled
into the snow. The wolf pack surrounded them!

Suddenly, a clawed hand seized one of the wolves. It was the Beast!

A wolf bit his arm and the Beast threw him against a tree. The pack retreated into the darkness.

FRIENDSHIP BLOSSOMS

Belle and Philippe helped the injured Beast back to the castle.

Belle tended to the Beast's wound. "Thank you for saving my life," she said gently.

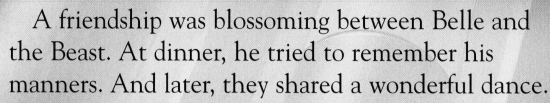

A friendship was blossoming between Belle and the Beast. At dinner, he tried to remember his manners. And later, they shared a wonderful dance. After they danced, the Beast asked Belle if she was happy.

"Yes," said Belle. "If only I could see my father."

The Beast brought Belle a magic mirror. When she wished to see her father, Maurice appeared in the glass, wandering lost in the forest.

"You must go to him. Take the mirror with you, so you can remember me," said the Beast sadly.

Belle left the castle. She brought her father home and lovingly cared for him. She told him about the Beast's kindness to her, and how he had let her go. Then there was a knock at the door.

49

Gaston had arrived with an angry crowd. "I'm here to take your crazy father to the asylum. He thinks he's seen a beast." Gaston would only release Maurice if Belle agreed to marry him.

When Belle used the magic mirror to show the Beast to the crowd, Gaston locked Belle and her father in their cellar. He set off to attack the Beast.

When Gaston's mob entered the castle, an army of dishes and furniture assaulted them. Gaston searched the halls until he found the Beast.

At that very moment, Belle escaped from
the cellar and began riding toward the castle!

Just as Belle and her father arrived, Gaston fired an arrow at the Beast.

"No!" sobbed Belle. She charged into the castle and ran up the stairs.

Belle had come back! With new hope, the Beast began to fight. When Belle reached them, the Beast had Gaston by the throat. "Let me go!" cried Gaston. The Beast felt sorry for Gaston and released him.

As the Beast embraced Belle, Gaston stabbed him in the back! The Beast let out a terrible roar, and Gaston tripped and fell off the balcony.

The Beast collapsed in Belle's arms.

"You came back," said the Beast. "At least I got to see you one last time." Belle began to cry. In the Beast's room, the last rose petal was about to fall. "No! Please . . . *please!*" said Belle. "I love you."

At Belle's words, the Beast's horrible claws turned into human hands, and his face grew smooth and fine. The spell was broken! "Belle, it's me," said the Prince, and they embraced.

Joyfully, all the enchanted objects in the castle returned to their human forms.

And as Belle and her prince shared a wonderful dance, she knew that her dreams of romance and adventure had all come true.